FEELINGS
Excitement

Tamra B. Orr

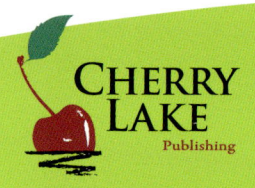

Published in the United States of America
by Cherry Lake Publishing
Ann Arbor, Michigan
www.cherrylakepublishing.com

Reading Adviser: Marla Conn MS, Ed., Literacy specialist, Read-Ability, Inc.

Photo Credits: © Andresr/Shutterstock Images, cover, 1; © Maria Uspenskaya/Shutterstock Images, 4; © mimagephotography/Shutterstock Images, 6; © supparsorn/Shutterstock Images, 8; © Studio 1One/Shutterstock Images, 10; © Yuliya Evstratenko/Shutterstock Images, 12; © MarcelaC/iStock Images, 14; © parinyabinsuk/Shutterstock Images, 16; © alvarez/iStock Images, 18; © Monkey Business Images/Shutterstock Images, 20

Copyright ©2017 by Cherry Lake Publishing
All rights reserved. No part of this book may be reproduced or utilized in any form or by any means without written permission from the publisher.

Library of Congress Cataloging-in-Publication Data

Names: Orr, Tamra, author.
Title: Excitement / Tamra B. Orr.
Description: Ann Arbor : Cherry Lake Publishing, 2016. | Series: Feelings | Audience: K to Grade 3. | Includes bibliographical references and index.
Identifiers: LCCN 2015048093| ISBN 9781634710428 (hardcover) | ISBN 9781634711418 (pdf) | ISBN 9781634712408 (pbk.) | ISBN 9781634713399 (ebook)
Subjects: LCSH: Emotions--Juvenile literature.
Classification: LCC BF511 .O67 2016 | DDC 152.4--dc23
LC record available at https://lccn.loc.gov/2015048093

Cherry Lake Publishing would like to acknowledge the work of The Partnership for 21st Century Learning. Please visit www.p21.org for more information.

Printed in the United States of America
Corporate Graphics

Table of Contents

5   A Special Calendar
9   Counting the Days
13 So Hard to Wait
17 Grandma's Here!

22 Find Out More
22 Glossary
23 Home and School Connection
24 Index
24 About the Author

What do you think this girl is excited about?

A Special Calendar

I pick up the big pencil.

The day is over. I will mark it off on my special **calendar**.

6

I can't stop smiling. I am so **excited**!

How can you tell this girl is excited?

Counting the Days

I have been counting the days for weeks now.

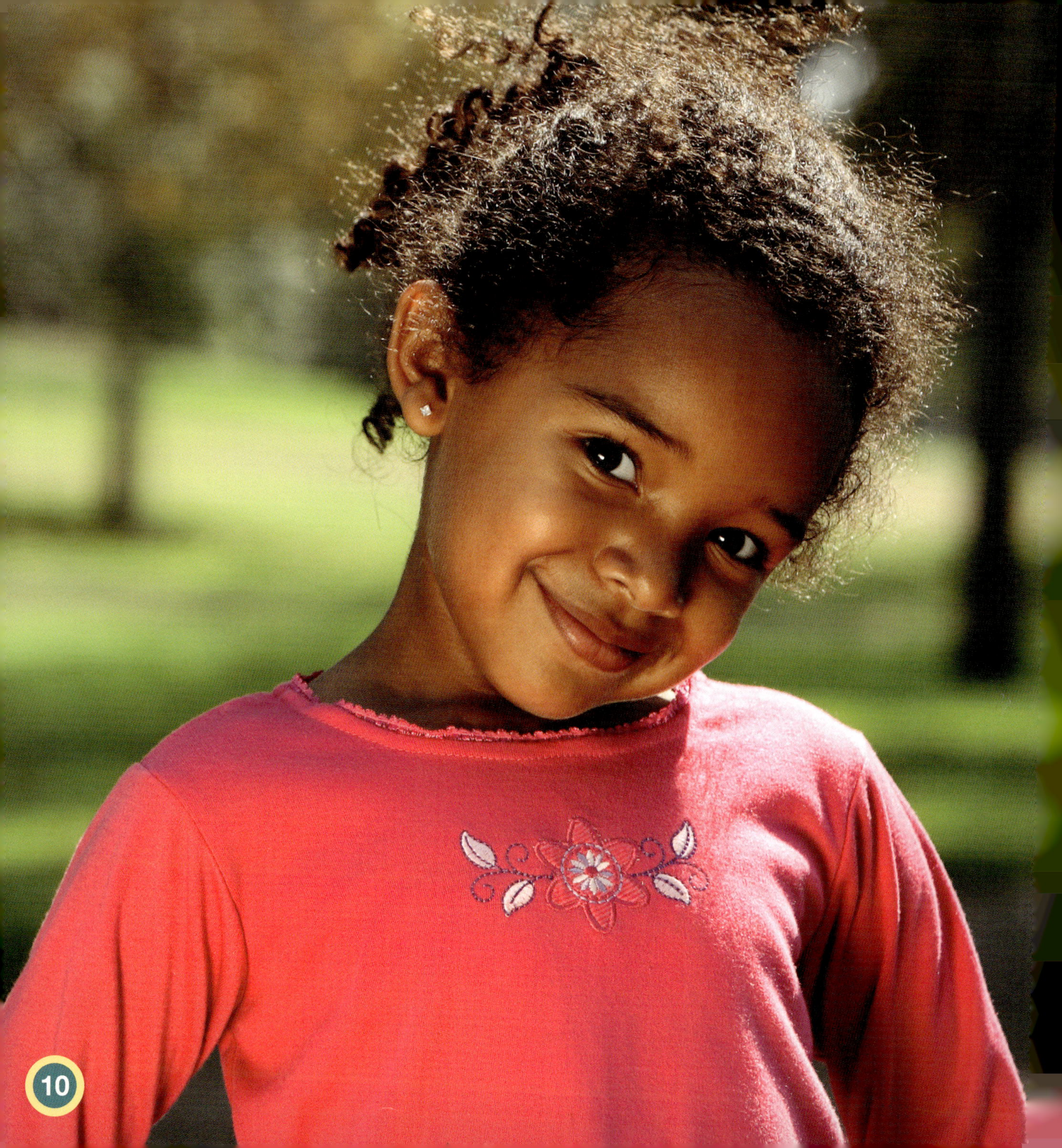

I am crossing each one off until Grandma gets here.

It is getting closer every day.

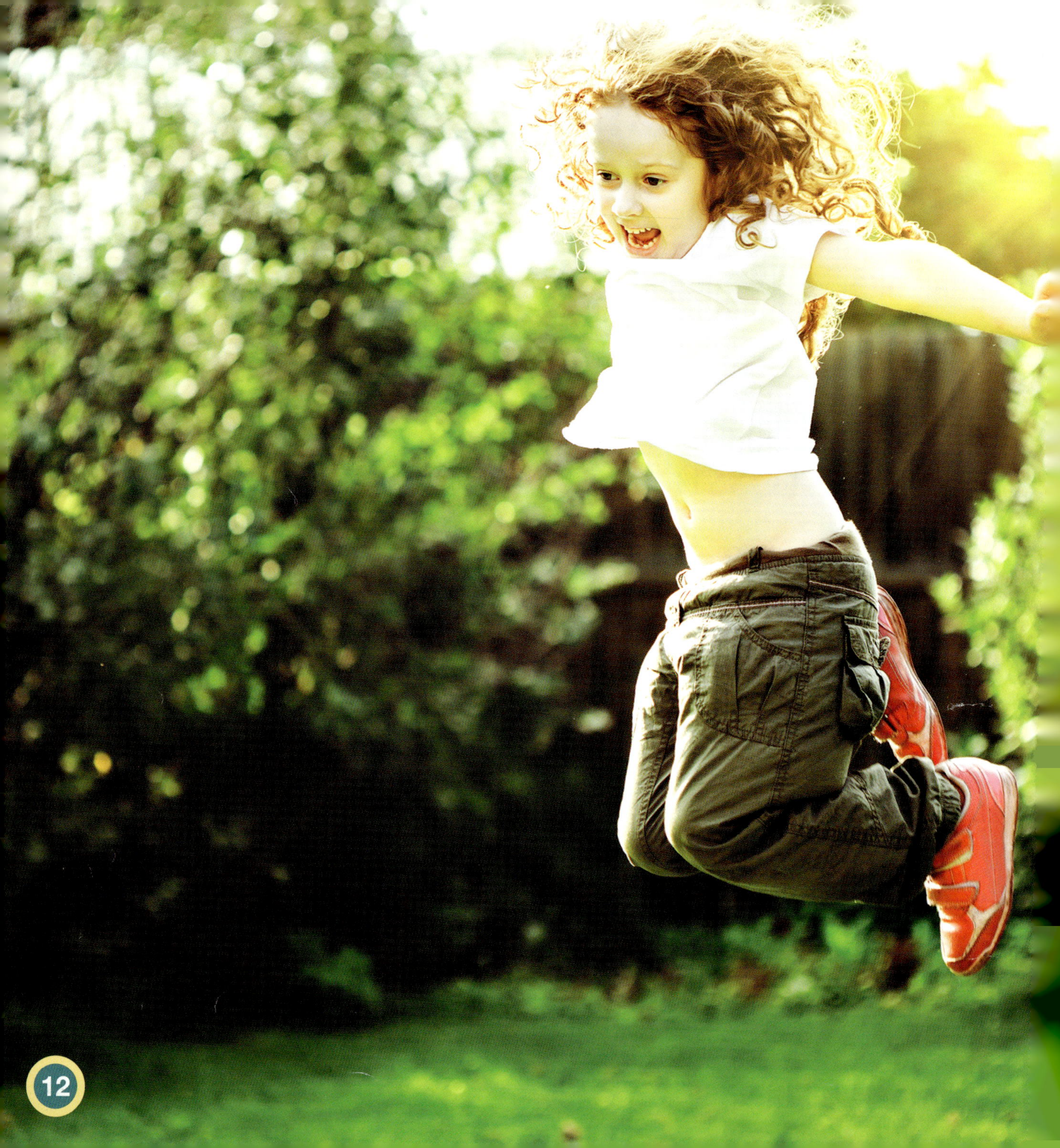

So Hard to Wait

It is hard to wait. I miss Grandma.

I get so excited, I jump up and down.

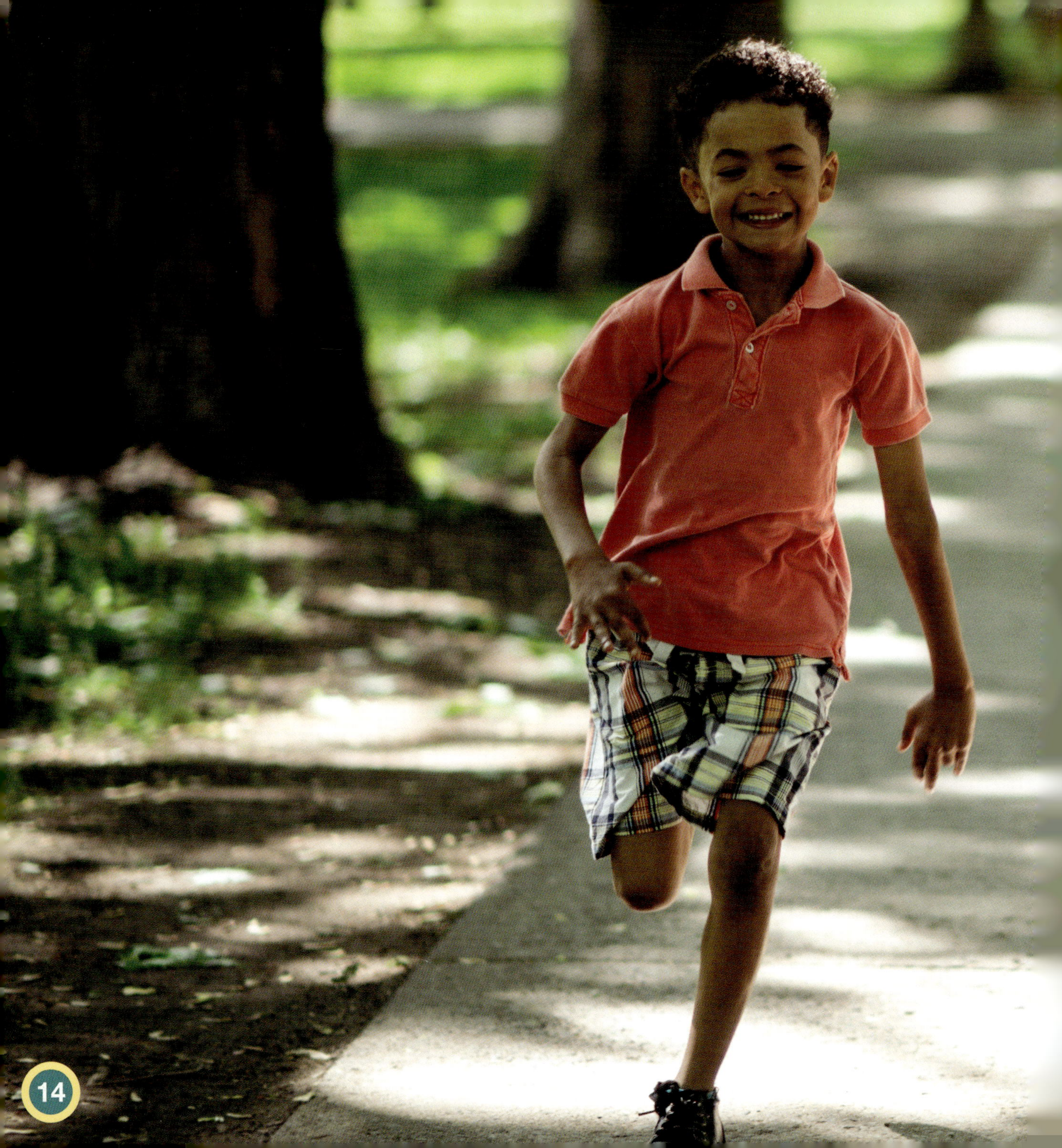

Sometimes I run and **shout**.
I can't sit still!

16

Grandma's Here!

We are at the **airport**. I am holding flowers.

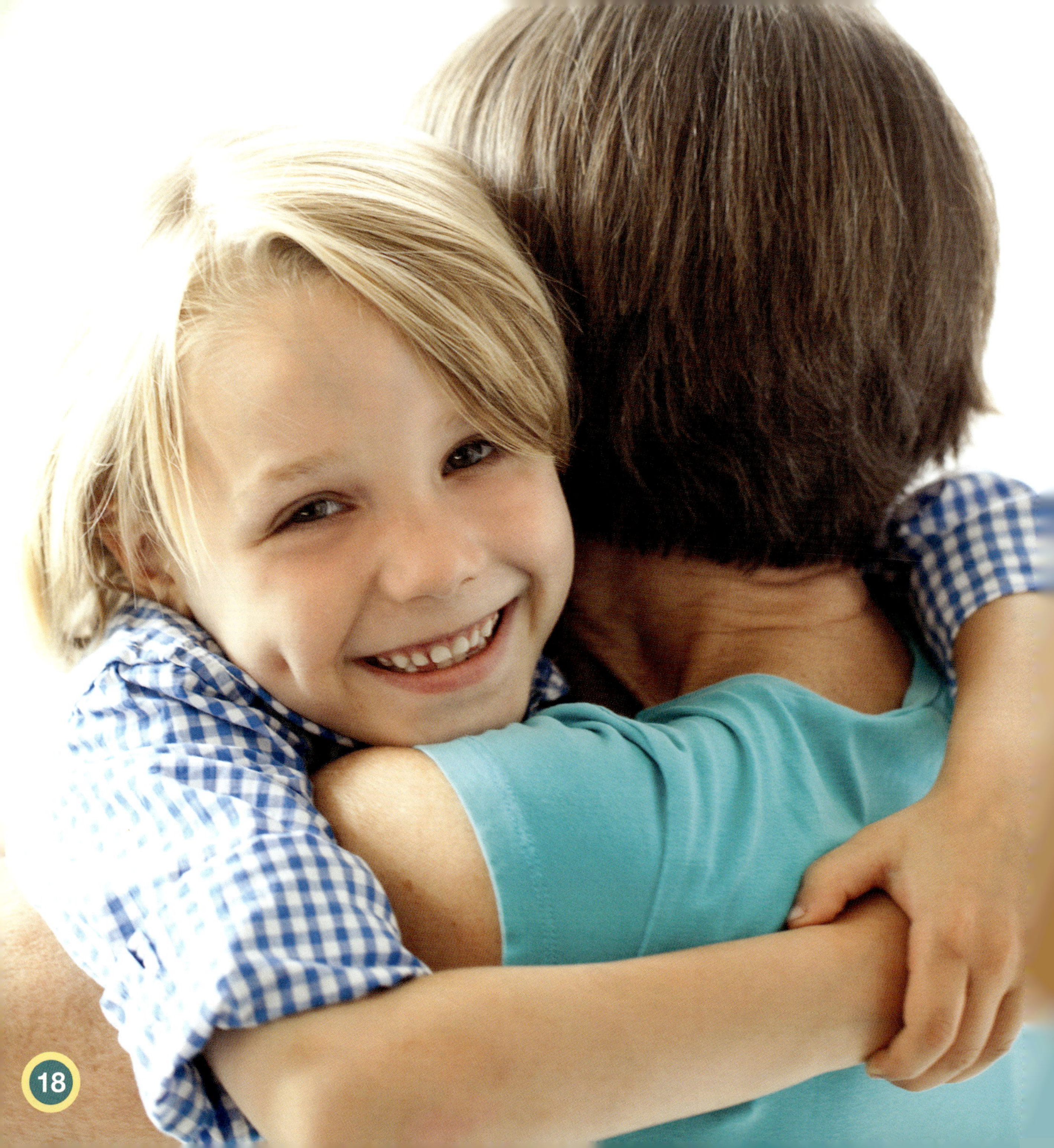

I can't stop moving.

Oh, I see her! I run, and we hug.

20

Look! Her excitement is as great as mine!

Find Out More

Corr, Christopher, and Quentin Samuel. *Why Is Everybody So Excited?* London: Zero to Ten Children's Books, 2001.

Nemiroff, Marc. *Shy Spaghetti and Excited Eggs: A Kid's Menu of Feelings*. Washington, DC: Magination Press, 2011.

Nourigat, Paul. *Earning Excitement*. Portland, OR: FarBeyond Publishing, 2012.

Glossary

airport (AIR-port) a place where people come and go on airplanes

calendar (KAL-uhn-dur) a chart of the days, weeks, and months of the year

excited (ik-SITE-id) a feeling of happiness about something that is going to happen

shout (SHOUT) to talk very loudly

Home and School Connection

Use this list of words from the book to help your child become a better reader. Word games and writing activities can help beginning readers reinforce literacy skills.

airport	every	holding	see
and	excited	hug	shout
are	excitement	jump	sit
been	flowers	look	smiling
big	for	mark	sometimes
calendar	get	mine	special
can't	gets	miss	still
closer	getting	moving	stop
counting	grandma	now	the
crossing	great	off	until
day	hard	over	wait
days	have	pencil	we
down	her	pick	weeks
each one	here	run	will

Index

airport, 17

calendar, 5

day, 5, 9, 11

flowers, 17

grandma, 11, 13

jump, 13

pencil, 5

shout, 15
smiling, 7

weeks, 9

About the Author

Tamra Orr has written more than 400 books for young people. The only thing she loves more than writing books is reading them. She lives in beautiful Portland, Oregon, with her husband, four children, dog, and cat. She says that she has gone to the airport many times to greet people with hugs and flowers.